Lucky's Mountain

DIANNE MAYCOCK

ORCA BOOK PUBLISHERS

Library and Archives Canada Cataloguing in Publication

Maycock, Dianne

Lucky's mountain / written by Dianne Maycock.

ISBN 978-1-55143-682-1

I. Title.

PS8626.A932L84 2007 jC813'.6 C2006-907016-4

First published in the United States, 2007
Library of Congress Control Number: 2006940393

Summary: Forced to leave the only home she has ever known, Maggie must
also find a good home for her beloved dog, Lucky.

Orca Book Publishers gratefully acknowledges the support for its publishing programs
provided by the following agencies: the Government of Canada through the Book
Publishing Industry Development Program and the Canada Council for the Arts,
and the Province of British Columbia through the
BC Arts Council and the Book Publishing Tax Credit.

Typesetting by Christine Toller
Cover artwork by Simon Ng

ORCA BOOK PUBLISHERS
PO Box 5626, STN. B
VICTORIA, BC CANADA
V8R 6S4

ORCA BOOK PUBLISHERS
PO Box 468
CUSTER, WA USA
98240-0468

www.orcabook.com
Printed and bound in Canada.

10 09 08 07 • 4 3 2 1

*For Gilly, who led me joyously into the world
of children's books all over again.*

Acknowledgments

Thanks to Ellen Schwartz, who believed in me from the very beginning; my husband John, for his unwavering support; and Sarah Harvey, for guiding me cheerfully and patiently through the process of revision.

Chapter One

The day the letter finally arrived, Maggie ran all the way home from the post office without stopping once. Not even to gobble a handful of the ripe red huckleberries that dotted the bushes along the trail.

She glanced down at the envelope again, wishing desperately that she could just rip it open. But even with Auntie Horse's frilly handwriting, there was no mistaking Mama's name—Mrs. Thelma Sullivan.

Lucky stopped in his tracks and turned to gaze back at her with a lopsided grin, as if they were playing go-go-stop. It was one of their favorite games, along with hide-and-seek, except that Lucky wasn't very good at the hiding part. But what he lacked in skill, he more than made up for with boisterous tail-wagging and never ever arguing about the rules.

By the time she joined him on the back porch, they were both panting. "No fair," Maggie said breathlessly. "How come you never let me win?"

Lucky grinned harder, and his plumy tail swished back and forth against the wood. When he was sitting like that it was impossible to tell that he wasn't just the same as any other dog. For the hundredth time Maggie wondered—did he know? Deep inside his doggy brain, did he understand?

Falling to her knees, she flung her arms around his neck. "Good boy," she whispered, "you're a good good boy." She nuzzled her cheek against his soft golden ear and released him. "You stay here, okay? I'll be back soon."

Lucky nodded to show that he understood. He *did* nod, all the time, even if Mama and Maggie's sister Elly refused to believe it. Maggie and Pa were the only ones who had always believed in Lucky's special gifts. For a precious instant Pa's face floated in front of her, wearing the expression she loved the very best—that part-sweet, part-wicked smile, matched with a twinkle in the eyes.

Blinking the image away, she scrambled to her feet and yanked open the back door. "It's here, Mama. Can I open it?"

"*May* I." Mama corrected Maggie without raising her eyes from the flowered china teacup she was wrapping in newsprint. Her face was flushed and her usually spotless apron was streaked with dirt. "Go ahead."

Suddenly Maggie's heart was thudding against her ribs. This was only the most important letter she was ever going to read! With trembling fingers she ripped at the envelope and unfolded the plain white paper inside.

"Well?" Elly said. She was hunched over the oak chest, arranging paper-wrapped bundles into careful piles. Everything Elly did was careful or tidy or *sensible*, as Mama would say. The exact opposite of Maggie, as Mama said too. "What does she say?"

"She says…" Auntie Horse's writing, crammed onto a single sheet, was difficult to read. "She says 'No'!" Maggie wailed. "I hate her!" Crumpling the letter in her fist, she hurled it at the floor.

"Margaret Sullivan." Mama's voice was as hard and sharp as a nail. "Pick…it…up. This instant. And read it aloud. I want to hear what she has to say."

As Maggie fumbled to smooth out the wad of paper, a tear plopped onto her hand. She shook her head angrily. Why did these stupid tears have to keep coming all the time? She was sick of tears.

And stupid old Auntie Horseface was *not* going to make her cry.

She drew a shuddery breath and let it out slowly. "'Dear Thelma and children, Given the circumstances, I hope you are keeping as well as can be expected. The weather here has been unseasonably hot, and we could do with a good hard rain. My arthritis is getting worse, making life difficult, and I am looking forward to your help. There will be plenty for the girls to do. Tell Margaret that I am sorry b-but," Maggie bit savagely on her bottom lip, "there is simply no place for a dog in a city boarding house. A cat might be useful, to help with the loathsome rats that roam everywhere.'"

Maggie gazed defiantly at Mama. "She's the meanest old nag that ever lived. I wish…I wish an old rat would bite her!"

Mama frowned at her. Her face, once so soft and pretty, looked almost ugly now. "Enough," she said sharply. "We have no time for your tantrums."

The tears pricked again, for an instant, before Maggie scowled them away. If Mama could be a nail, *she* could be a giant steel spike. For what seemed like an hour, she and Mama locked gazes.

Finally Mama heaved a loud sigh. When she spoke, her voice had softened. "I know it's hard, Maggie, but your Aunt Hortense is right. We simply can't take Lucky with us."

Elly stopped working to gaze up at her. "You'll just have to find him a good home here," she said matter-of-factly. "Why don't you ask Mrs. Cameron if you can make an announcement at school?"

Leave Lucky behind? Her very best friend in the whole entire world? "I always knew you hated him!" she yelled, flinging the letter at Elly as she stumbled toward the door.

And there he was, scrambling to meet her, his big brown eyes melting with concern. And love.

He was the only one left who really truly loved her.

Chapter Two

Mrs. Cameron rapped sharply on her desk with the pointer. "Hands folded, eyes front." She waited for the class to settle, her lips pressed into a single narrow line. Then she nodded at Maggie. "Come forward, Margaret."

If only there were some other way! But Mama wouldn't even listen, thought Maggie. Slowly she stood up and walked to the front of the room. Clenching her jaw so tightly it hurt, she gazed out at the sea of faces. Not a single one of those lumps staring back at her could possibly love Lucky the way that she did. Not even Abigail, who was smiling at her encouragingly from the middle of the room.

The forty boys and girls who were packed like sardines into the junior schoolhouse were seated by grade, with the little ones on the right and the grade sevens clumped together on the far left. Maggie always thought that it made the room look strangely lopsided, as if it might suddenly tilt to one side.

"We're waiting, Margaret," said Mrs. Cameron.

Maggie blinked. "Sorry," she mumbled. She sucked in a deep breath. "We're moving away at the end of the month and we can't take Lucky."

Don't you dare cry, she told herself fiercely. Not once had Maggie Sullivan ever cried at school. Not even when Mrs. Cameron had smacked her with the pointer, leaving angry red welts on her palm, and then made her stand in the corner all afternoon.

When the whole thing was really Jock Webster's fault.

Or the time she'd tumbled out of the giant fir and broken her ankle. Abigail was the one who cried, and she hadn't even gotten hurt!

Maggie fixed her gaze on the blackened stovepipe that disappeared into the ceiling at the back of the room. "Lucky's a wonderful dog. He's smart and funny and loyal. I want to ask if anyone will take him."

She stood straight as a soldier, waiting.

Not a single hand went up.

Whispers hissed around the room like snakes. Jock Webster, slouched in his seat at the back of the room, muttered something behind his hand to Davy McBain.

Davy smirked back at him.

Those fatheads! Anger flashed through Maggie's head like a lightning bolt, scorching away all thought of tears.

"We all wish you luck in finding him a good home," Mrs. Cameron said quietly. She raised her voice. "All right, class, you may leave for lunch. Walking, please."

While the room around Maggie swirled into motion, her own body had stiffened to stone. So no one wanted Lucky? Well, *good*, because not one of them was fit to lick his paws.

And what if somebody *had* wanted him? What would she have done then?

"Are you okay?"

Maggie jumped. Abigail's round face was puckered with distress. "I'm fine," she snapped. And before Abigail could say another word, Maggie started marching toward the cloakroom. "Come on."

As soon as she stepped out into the warm spring sunshine, a dozen heads turned to stare. Mind your own business! she wanted to scream. Instead she gazed straight at the tallest treetop and half-stalked, half-sprinted across the yard toward the fallen log that she and Abigail had claimed as their own. Tucked under the cedars, cushiony with moss, it was their own private eating spot.

Abigail hoisted herself up onto the log and opened her round metal lunch pail. Her lips parted with anticipation.

Maggie slumped beside her, watching listlessly. There'd been a time—it seemed like years ago now—when this had been her second-favorite part of the day. Which yummy treat had Mrs. Bryson packed for Abigail? It didn't really matter; Maggie loved them all: the iced lemon squares, the gooey chocolate brownies, the bumbleberry crumble cake.

But lately nothing tasted right. It had gotten so bad that Mama had even taken to offering her waffles for breakfast, or bread dripping with honey, in place of the dreaded oatmeal.

Never in a million years would that have happened...before.

Abigail bit hungrily into her roast pork sandwich. "I'm sorry about Lucky," she mumbled. "I'd take him, you know I would, but Mum says dogs smell and they have fleas." She darted a glance at Maggie.

"Lucky doesn't have fleas!" Maggie yanked savagely at a chunk of moss. "And I *like* his smell." She flung the moss into the bushes.

"I know," Abigail said quickly, "but—"

"Hey, Sullivan!" Jock was swaggering toward them, flanked by Davy McBain and Jimmy Ellis. "If you think anyone's gonna take that ugly old gimp, you're even loonier than Crazy Louie." He crossed his eyes and waggled his tongue from side to side.

Jimmy and Davy snorted with laughter.

Flashing a smug look at Maggie, Jock darted toward the bushes and snatched up a long skinny branch. "I know what *I'd* do with him," he said, pointing the branch at Jimmy. "Bang!"

Jimmy clutched his chest and dropped to the dirt, giggling hysterically.

Fury whipped through Maggie's head. "Shut up!" she screeched as she hurled herself straight at Jock. Raising her lunch box, she smashed it as hard as she could into his left ear.

"Owwwwww!" he howled, stumbling backward. "You little witch!"

Abigail scrambled off the log and grabbed Maggie's arm. "Come on," she cried, dragging Maggie toward the safety of the school.

Chapter Three

When Maggie finally emerged from the classroom at 3:15, Abigail was sitting on the porch steps, giggling about something with Jessie.

Maggie's frown deepened. Was it her imagination or did Jessie Ramsey seem to be everywhere lately, buzzing around Abigail like a pesky fruit fly around a juicy plum.

Jessie's buggy eyes gleamed with curiosity. "So did Jock tell Mrs. Cameron what you did to him?" she demanded. "What did she say?"

Jessie *knew*? Maggie stared at Abigail in disbelief. For as long as she could remember, Abigail had been her very best friend. Her loyal best friend. And now loyalty had just winged away on the mountain breeze.

Abigail's cheeks looked like fat overripe tomatoes. "Sorry," she murmured. "I didn't mean…it just…I'm sorry," she repeated.

Maggie stared at her for a moment longer and shrugged.

Abigail scrambled to her feet and leaned in close to Maggie. "*Did* she find out? About…?" She tapped her left ear.

Maggie shook her head. Jock Webster might be creepier than a rattlesnake, but he was no tattletale. The only thing he hated worse than school was schoolteachers. "She just wanted to talk about school stuff," she said, pulling a face. About the spelling test, to be exact—the one where Maggie got only four right out of ten. And about her seven careless arithmetic mistakes. Careless was Mrs. Cameron's word, but Maggie had to admit that it fit. Right now she couldn't care less if she was failing every subject.

"What stuff?" Jessie said, standing up beside Abigail.

Maggie flashed her a none-of-your-business look, and then she turned to Abigail. "You ready to go?" she said pointedly. She and Abigail had been walking home from school together since the first day of grade one.

Abigail's mouth opened and closed. Her gaze flicked to Jessie.

Jessie held up a nickel. "She's going with me," she announced smugly. "To the store."

"I've got money too," Abigail said quickly. "Why don't you come with us and I'll buy you a peppermint twist."

What's the matter, Abby? Feeling guilty? thought Maggie. Peppermint twists were Maggie's absolute favorite, and Abigail knew it. But with Jessie there, a peppermint twist would taste like chalk. "No, thank you," Maggie said stiffly. "I have to help at home." It wasn't exactly a lie. Mama was bound and determined to leave the house cleaner than she'd found it when they'd first moved in.

Anyway, she wanted—needed—to see Lucky. *He* was still loyal at least. And how many more days would she be able to see him and smell him and bury her face in his fur?

"I have to go," she muttered. Thrusting past Jessie, she leapt off the porch and started sprinting across the schoolyard.

Apart from Jessie's "Hey, watch it," neither girl bothered to call after her, not even to say good-bye. Maggie kicked savagely at a pinecone. So what? She could live without Abigail. But how was she going to live without Lucky?

Suddenly she was hurtling along the trail like Granite Creek during spring thaw, leaping over tree roots and slapping at the branches that attacked her bare arms.

As she neared the clearing she heard the *clink-rattle* of the chain, followed by excited barking. Lucky bounded forward, and then he jerked to a halt as the collar bit deep into his neck. You'd think he'd remember about the chain, he hated it so much, but his face wore its usual comical look of surprise.

"Stay," Maggie called. "Sit." She hated the chain too, but it was meant to keep him from following her to school. Not that he needed a chain anymore. He really didn't, but Mama simply wouldn't budge. Ever since that time he'd galloped right into the classroom, hot on the trail of a panicky squirrel. It turned out that Mrs. Cameron didn't like squirrels. Or dogs. At least not in the classroom.

As she knelt to unclip him, he scrubbed her face with his tongue and waggled his whole body as if he were a rambunctious puppy. Maggie ruffled his fur. "I missed you too."

He sank back on his haunches and lifted his right paw.

Solemnly Maggie shook it. "And how are you today, Mr. Sullivan?"

Lucky barked the way he always did, his grin stretching from ear to ear. What a contrast from the day she'd first seen him. The day that Pa had stumbled into the yard cradling a bloody bundle of fur. Caught in a cougar trap, he'd told her. Half-dead from hunger and obviously not missed.

She and Pa had headed straight for Doc Brixton's. The dog would live, he'd told them. And get around just fine on three legs.

That was the day she'd named him Lucky.

Then, on her birthday, Pa had given her the best present in the whole entire world. "Margaret Elizabeth," he'd said, "this dog is yours now. I know you'll take good care of him."

And I will! I will take good care of you! Maggie thought as she rubbed her cheek against Lucky's silky ear.

The back door swung open. "I thought I heard you out here." Mama stepped out onto the porch and rested her arms on the weather-bleached wooden rail. Underneath the gray scarf she'd tied over her hair, her face looked tired and old.

Something clutched at Maggie's heart. Mama? Old?

"So, how did it go at school?" Mama said. "Does anyone want him?"

In that instant her heart became as stiff and hard as a brick. Here she'd actually been feeling sorry for Mama, when all Mama cared about was getting rid of a pest. She didn't care a hoot if Lucky lived or died!

And what about Pa? If Mama *really* cared about Pa, wouldn't she find a way to stay here? How could she bear to leave him behind? Maggie was about to snap something back when an idea popped into her head. For weeks now she'd been going along blindly, stupidly, with everything Mama had said and done.

Well, not anymore.

She jumped to her feet. "I'll be back before dinner."

Mama's eyebrows lifted into perfect black arches. "What? Where are you going?"

But Maggie was already sprinting across the clearing with Lucky bounding eagerly at her heels.

Chapter Four

Instead of heading toward the school, Maggie veered to the right at the giant pine and took the path toward town. A faint sweet scent from the wild rose bushes wafted through the air.

Two summers ago, she and Pa had picked a whole bucketful of rose petals, pricking their fingers to bits, after he'd read about the Indians using them for jam. But somehow they'd never gotten around to jam-making, and Mama had eventually tossed out the whole soggy mess.

At the end of the trail she emerged into warm sunshine and turned onto the main road, which was really just an extra-wide trail used by the company trucks. Luckily the mine office was at the top of the hill, the opposite direction from Number Three Mine. Not even for Lucky could she bring herself to go anywhere near that place. Never again.

What was that? Maggie stopped in her tracks, listening hard. She shook her head. It's not real, she told herself, it's not real. But she couldn't shake away the sound of the whistle blast she'd heard that day. Instead of the three quick bursts that were used to call the next shift of miners in to work, there had been only a single spine-chilling shriek. *Trouble*! it signaled. *Trouble at the mine*! *Come quick*!

In her mind's eye, she could see herself racing along the road with Mama and Elly, their faces white as paint. Waiting with the others. Not talking, not moving, just waiting to see if Pa was ever going to come out again. Praying for a glimpse of his coal-blackened face.

A dark and horrible feeling of emptiness washed over Maggie like a giant wave. It was as if the world around her had suddenly vanished, taking with it the sun, the sky and the grass beneath her feet. She struggled to breathe.

Lucky's damp nose thrust against her hand. He whimpered softly.

Maggie gazed down at him, still in a daze.

He thrust again, harder, and gave a sharp *woof*.

Maggie's fingers brushed his forehead, caressing the silken fur. "You're right," she whispered, "no more thinking." She raised her voice. "It's time to *do* something, isn't it?"

Lucky nodded.

Maggie ran the tips of her fingers along her braids—they felt all right. Mama yanked them so tight every morning that they hardly ever came undone. Then she peered down at her dress. Uh-oh. A purplish blob of dried jelly stained the light blue fabric just below the waist. "Here," she said, pointing to it. "Lick."

Lucky looked at the blob, then up at her, his head cocked to one side.

"Yes, I do mean it. Lick!"

A second later his rough pink tongue was scrubbing at the stain. Leaving behind an even bigger wet splotch. Never mind, it would soon dry in the sun. "Good boy. Now let's go."

It was odd how the Coalworks building looked just like her own house. Except for the paint. Unlike most of the buildings in town, which were just plain unpainted wood, the mine company office was a crisp clean white. The windows, yawning wide in the heat, were trimmed in dark green.

Maggie led Lucky to a cluster of spindly firs that hugged one side of the building. "Lie down." He licked her hand and obediently lowered his stomach onto the dirt.

"I'll be back soon. Stay. " Maggie took three strides toward the door and stopped. Now that she was here, her brilliant idea didn't seem so brilliant anymore. What on earth was she going to say? Butterflies fluttered in her stomach.

Lucky gave a short sharp bark. Maggie turned to see him scrambling to his feet. He was staring at her anxiously.

"It's okay." She pointed to the trees. "Lie down. And stay." She waited until he sank back down, and then she turned and marched toward the door. All her doubts had vanished.

She could do *anything* for Lucky.

A short skinny lady, older than Mama, was standing behind the counter where the men lined up to collect their pay. Behind her were two rooms: one with its door half open, and the other with its door firmly closed. Maggie stared at the closed door, wondering for a moment if it concealed the huge iron safe. Pa had told her about that safe and how just before payday it was stuffed with hundreds, even thousands, of dollars.

Payday, the fourth Friday of every month, was a very important event in town, and Maggie had heard plenty of stories over the years. How a lot of the single men rushed straight from the office to the bunk-house, stopping only to change out of their filthy work clothes and into their poker-playing duds. How one eager fellow named Jerry Flynn always wore the same pair of "lucky" silk pants. Games like rap rummy and blackjack ran day and night all weekend long. Maggie had been intrigued to learn that some of the men didn't even stop gambling to sleep or to eat.

Things were different for the men with families, who often didn't get much of a paycheck at all. Since Coalworks owned the one and only store in town, everyone had to shop there, and purchases were docked from the men's pay. Maggie had once over-heard Pa telling Mama about Mr. Bryson "hitting the roof" when he opened his envelope and found a check for eighty-seven cents. Then Mama had told Pa how lucky he was to be married to her instead of Mrs. Bryson, who loved nothing better than shop-ping. And then Pa had swept Mama into his arms and murmured something that had set Mama to giggling like a six-year-old.

"Yes?" said a disapproving voice.

Maggie blinked. The lady was peering at her over the top of her wire-rim glasses.

"I…" Maggie cleared her throat. "I'd like to see Mr. Winters, please."

The lady, who wore a gray dress that matched the color of her tightly waved hair, frowned. "Mr. Winters is very busy right now." Her voice sounded just the way she looked, stiff as a dried-up rag. "Can I help you?"

"No!" Maggie burst out.

The lady's face twisted as if she had just smelled a skunk. "I beg your pardon?"

Maggie took a deep breath, let it out and forced her lips into a smile. "I'm sorry, ma'am. It's just that I really *need* to see Mr. Winters."

The lady didn't smile back. "And I just told you that he's very busy."

"I'm Margaret Sullivan, Jack Sullivan's daughter." Jack Sullivan's daughter. Just saying those words out loud made her lips start to quiver. Hastily she clamped them together.

The lady was staring at Maggie with the expression of someone who wasn't sure what to say. "I…oh. Very well, wait here."

She turned, knocked on the door behind her and went in.

Chapter Five

Mr. Winters was seated at a large wooden desk whose surface was hidden by untidy heaps of papers and long cardboard tubes. Also cluttering the desktop was a pen and pencil set, a clock in a shiny black frame, and a green tin of Risley's Toffees.

The head of Coalworks was a beefy dark-haired man who was stuffed uncomfortably between the armrests of his chair. With his bushy black eyebrows and hairy arms, he looked like one of the bears that roamed the mountain every summer—a bear that could chew up a person and spit out her bones.

"Good afternoon," he said, his voice booming around the room. "Please, sit." He waved a hand at one of the two straight-backed chairs facing his desk.

"Thank you, sir," Maggie mumbled, perching on the edge of the chair. She sat ramrod straight, as Mama had taught her, and rubbed her palms nervously on her dress. Was this man as fierce on the inside as he looked on the outside? Could she make him understand?

"Did your mother send you?" Mr. Winters asked abruptly. "I thought we'd finished with all the arrangements."

Maggie shook her head.

His lips tightened. "Then what can I do for you?" He glanced at the clock, then at a folder that lay open on his desk.

Maggie's throat was closed so tight it was as if her voice were locked inside. "I…I came to ask if you could please let us stay. In our house, I mean." Now that she'd started, the words came tumbling out. "We can earn the rent money. I know we can." She leaned forward eagerly. "If Mama could get a job at the store, maybe, and Elly could work at the post office?"

"Now hold on a minute." Mr. Winters raised a massive hand. "Your mother didn't say one word to me about wanting to stay. In fact I got the idea that she wanted to hightail it out of here as quick as she could." The thick eyebrows bristled menacingly at Maggie.

A wave of frustration washed over her, mixed with a feeling of panic. How could she make him understand, this gruff impatient man who seemed so different from

Pa? She took a deep breath and looked him in the eye. "Pa…my father loved this place. He said most mining towns are so *ugly,* and being up here was like being close to heaven." She leaned toward him, clasping her hands together. "He wouldn't want us to leave, I know he wouldn't."

Had his face softened, just a little?

"And all the things we…we…" The stupid tears were pricking again, but she blinked them away. "Baseball and skating, and those big bobsleds that you bought?"

He nodded.

"And the giant Christmas tree in the square? And the sing-alongs? We had so much fun."

Mr. Winters nodded again. "I set out to make this a good place for families. Right from the start." His lips curved in a satisfied smile.

Maggie's heart leapt. He *did* understand. Did this mean he was going to let them stay? "Then you'll help?"

But his head was already shaking a no, and his face had hardened into its businesslike mask. "I couldn't let you have the house, even if your mother wanted to stay. I've got new men coming in, and their families need somewhere to live."

New men? Taking Pa's place? That's all he cared about, his stupid old mine. He didn't care about the Sullivans at all! Maggie sprang to her feet. "But I *told* you. Pa loved it here and so do I, and," her voice rose, "what about Lucky?"

"Lucky?" The eyebrows drew together in a single black line.

"My dog. Pa gave him to me specially, to take care of," Maggie said desperately. "I *have* to take care of him!"

"Now look." Planting his hands on the desktop, Mr. Winters thrust himself to his feet. "I've tried to be patient."

"We can't take Lucky with us," Maggie burst out, her voice practically a shout. She had to make him understand! "Auntie Horse said we couldn't keep him at the boarding house."

"I've got a business to run here and people to take care of."

"Like you took care of Pa?" Maggie cried. "Your stupid mine *killed* him, and now you're going to kill my dog!" An ear-splitting volley of barks erupted from the other side of the door, and Lucky catapulted into the room. Teeth bared in a snarl, he growled at Mr. Winters as if he really were a bear.

"Come back here!" screeched the lady, rushing in after him.

Lucky reared onto his hind leg, his front paws scrabbling at the edge of the desk. The green tin crashed to the floor, sending toffees flying everywhere. Barking thundered around the room.

Mr. Winters snatched up a tube and whacked Lucky's head.

"Stop it!" Maggie shrieked. She grabbed a pile of folders and flung them in Mr. Winters' face.

Chapter Six

Just looking at the scummy grayish brown hunk of liver was enough to make Maggie gag. At least it didn't smell so bad now that it was cold.

"I hope you're eating in there," Mama called from the bedroom. She and Elly were sorting clothes, deciding which ones to throw out. Maggie, who was supposed to be helping, was still slumped at the kitchen table, trying to finish her least favorite dinner in the whole entire world.

Fried liver and mushy peas.

Mama served liver once a week, which was once a week too often in Maggie's opinion. But whenever she complained, Mama would launch into the same boring speech. Didn't Maggie realize how lucky she was to be eating liver at all? Didn't she know that the country was in the middle of a great depression, and lots of children were practically starving? Children who would give their right arms to eat liver and peas every single night of the week?

By then Maggie would be wriggling in her seat, trying not to scowl. Mama hated scowls.

One time Pa had chimed in too, his voice uncharacteristically stern. "Your mother's right," he'd said. "Compared to most families right now, we're at the top of the heap. I've got one of the few decent jobs around, we've got plenty of food, and Coalworks has given us a pretty nice roof over our heads. You, young lady, have a very good life." He had stared hard at Maggie for a moment before flashing her a wink. "Don't tell your ma," he'd whispered, leaning in close, "but liver's never been one of my favorites either."

She heaved a sigh and poked sharply with her fork at a clump of peas. Sometimes, if she were in an especially good mood, Mama didn't make her clean her plate, but tonight wasn't one of those nights. "How could you run off like that?" she'd demanded when Maggie had finally arrived home. "Do you think it's fair for you to be out playing somewhere while Elly and I have been slaving away since dawn?"

Thank goodness Mama didn't know what had

really happened. "Get out of my office," Mr. Winters had thundered, "and take that mongrel with you!"

Maggie felt sick to her stomach thinking about it.

She had just speared a single pea with her fork to be able to say she *was* eating, when she heard a soft whine. Maggie glanced over her shoulder and slid noiselessly out of her chair. Slowly, carefully, she turned the doorknob and cracked open the door.

A furry head pushed eagerly at the crack. Lucky whined again, louder this time.

"Shhh," Maggie hissed, glancing behind her again. "You know you can't come in."

Lucky gazed up at her with pleading eyes, his tail flapping like a hawk's wing. Maggie shook her head. "I can't let you in," she whispered, "but I've got an idea." She pointed at him. "Sit."

"Maggie?" Mama's voice slashed through the thin plaster wall. "What's going on in there? Are you eating?"

Maggie froze. "Yes," she called back. "I'm almost finished."

"I'll be there in *one* minute," Mama said.

Maggie patted Lucky, who had sunk obediently onto his haunches. "Stay," she mouthed. Then she skidded over to the table, snatched the liver off her plate and dashed back to the door. She flung the liver into the yard.

Lucky hurtled after it as if he were chasing a sassy squirrel.

"Maggie?"

She was coming! Heart beating like a tom-tom, Maggie shut the door, raced to the sink and turned the water on full blast. "Just getting a drink," she said, gazing innocently at Mama.

"Oh." Mama looked at the plate, and her face softened. "Good. One more forkful of peas and you can be done."

A hot wave flooded Maggie's face. Lying to Mama was getting to be a habit. For an instant she felt guilty, but then she remembered—Mama *wasn't* her friend.

Luckily Mama was so busy talking that she didn't notice a thing. "I've put a pile of clothes on the bed. I want you to try them on and see which ones still fit."

A knock sounded at the front door.

"I'll get it," Maggie said eagerly. She rushed into the living room and flung open the door.

Standing on the front porch was Mr. Winters. He didn't look at all happy.

Chapter Seven

For one panic-stricken moment, Maggie thought about slamming the door in his face. But it was too late. "Mr. Winters," Mama was saying in a surprised voice. "Please come in."

Maggie's stomach heaved.

"Sit down, please." Mama showed him to the green-patterned armchair; then she perched across from him on the sofa. She slid her legs sideways and crossed them neatly at the ankles. "Are there more papers to sign?"

Maggie stood like a statue.

Mr. Winters looked every bit as uncomfortable crammed into the armchair as he had in his office chair. He gazed somberly at Mama. "No."

Maggie's heart was beating so fast that it felt as if her chest might explode. Mama was going to kill her!

If only she could run far, far away. She took a step toward the kitchen.

"Just a moment, young lady," Mr. Winters said. "What I have to say concerns you."

Maggie felt hot, then cold. Ice-cold.

"Concerns *Maggie*?" Mama's gaze whipped back and forth between Mr. Winters and Maggie, her face the picture of astonishment. Then her lips tightened. "You had better sit down," she said to Maggie, patting the sofa. "Right here."

Maggie's whole body felt frozen. She lurched forward and practically toppled onto the sofa. She didn't dare look at Mama or at Mr. Winters, so she gazed numbly at her feet. An enormous smear of dirt marred the snowy whiteness of her left sock. Hastily she tucked her left foot underneath the right.

Mr. Winters cleared his throat. "Since your daughter's visit this afternoon, I—"

"My daughter's *visit*?" Mama interrupted, breaking her number one rule of polite conversation. She looked even more astonished than before.

"She didn't tell you?"

Two heads turned as one, both of them staring straight at Maggie. Her own head was spinning. She was sure that she was going to faint.

"Just what have you been up to, Margaret?" Mama said in a steely voice.

"I…" Maggie's voice cracked.

Mr. Winters raised his hand like a stop sign. "Please, let me," he said firmly to Mama. "Now that I've had time to think about it, I realize that I may have been a little harsh with Margaret this afternoon." He shot a glance at Maggie, and then he turned to Mama again. "But I still can't see my way to letting you stay in the house."

"Stay? You asked him to let us stay? *Here*?" For an instant Mama's mouth gaped wide, her second breach of rules in less than a minute. Then, with a visible effort of will, she pulled herself together. She frowned at Maggie, her lips pinched into a hard narrow line.

Maggie couldn't move, couldn't breathe. What would Mama say? Or do? She cringed against the sofa like a mouse trapped by a cat.

Then, suddenly, something inside her snapped. So what if Mama was angry? She was angry too. And she had every right to be. "I had to ask him!" she cried. "Because you don't care about anybody but yourself!"

Mama's face bleached as white as her apron. "What did you say?"

34

"You don't care that I love it here and Pa loved it here and now I'm going to lose Lucky." Maggie burst into noisy sobs.

Mama sat like a stone.

It was Mr. Winters who acted. Pushing himself to the edge of his seat, he fished in his jacket pocket and thrust a crumpled handkerchief into Maggie's hand. "Here," he said gruffly as he turned to Mama. "Don't be too rough on her, Mrs. Sullivan. She's been through a bad time. You all have."

He was taking *her* side? Against Mama? Maggie's sob died in her throat.

Mama gave a funny whimper and then tears flooded her eyes. She lunged sideways and crushed Maggie in a fierce hug. "I'm sorry," she whispered. "I'm so sorry."

And then she rocked her, back and forth, back and forth.

As Maggie inhaled her mother's comforting lavender smell, it all came flooding back. This was Mama, the Mama who loved her. And the Mama that she loved. "Me too," she whispered.

Mr. Winters cleared his throat.

"Oh," Mama gasped. She released Maggie abruptly and scrambled to her feet. "I'll just go and freshen up." She rushed out of the room.

As soon as Mama was out of earshot, Mr. Winters spoke. "It sounds like we're all sorry." He rubbed his chin. "Including me."

Maggie gazed at him through swollen eyelids, exhaustion rolling over her like a truck. Was he saying that he was sorry for hitting Lucky? Did she forgive him? She was simply too tired to think.

"I have to go," Mr. Winters said, pushing himself to his feet, "but I came here to tell you I have an idea about your dog."

About *Lucky*? Maggie's lips parted in shock.

"Louie Jenkins. In Pig Valley. He'll take Lucky for you. Just tell him I sent you."

Louie Jenkins? Mr. Winters wanted her to give Lucky to a crazy man?

Chapter Eight

Lucky bounded through the low brush, a well-chewed branch dangling from his mouth. He dropped it at Maggie's feet and gave a proud bark.

Despite her mood, Maggie couldn't help smiling. "Yes, you are a clever boy." She picked up the branch by one end, trying to avoid the soggy bits. "Aren't you tired yet?"

She and Lucky had walked all the way across town, scrambled down Barnes' Hill and raced along Sunny Ridge trail to the clearing that overlooked the valley. At the far end of the cleared area lay the reservoir that held the town water supply. Pa had told her the pipes that snaked underground from the pump shed supplied water to every single building on the mountain. Including the houses. Coalworks prided itself on the fact that every home had running water, even though each man was expected to do his own plumbing.

Lucky barked impatiently, his tail swishing back and forth.

"All right, but this is the last one," she said with mock sternness. "Ready?" She raised the branch.

His body tensed.

"Go!" She flung it as hard as she could across the clearing.

Lucky shot off like a fox after a jackrabbit, hurling himself body and soul into the chase. He was every bit as good as any other dog, Maggie thought as she watched him. Better, even. If only other people could see it too. An image of Jock Webster and Davy McBain floated into her head. Angrily she shook it away, turned on her heel and marched toward the edge of the cliff.

The cliff, known as Sunny Ridge, plunged about five feet straight down before angling out into a steep, brush-covered slope with a thicket of pines at the bottom. Beyond the trees the slope flattened out for a bit, then plunged deep into the valley below. It reminded Maggie of a giant roller coaster.

She peered down into the valley. The view was breathtaking, an endless panorama of rippling green. The farther out she gazed, the softer the trees looked—

as soft and inviting as the plushest carpet. A strong gust of wind batted playfully at her dress. Pa had loved the wind up here. "Blows away the coal dust," he'd say, "and leaves the air clean as…"

"A new penny!" Maggie would shout. Or "Mama's kitchen floor!" Or "Lucky after his bath!"

Then Pa would look at her with that glint in his eyes and laugh out loud. And she would laugh too, for the sheer joy of things. And Lucky would bark like a crazy dog and dance his happy dance.

The branch thudded at her feet, and Lucky brushed comfortingly against her leg.

"Good boy," she whispered, snuggling her fingers into his warm fur. She took a deep breath, then forced herself to look up from the valley floor. Up, up, up until she spotted a large flat patch of brown. Pig Valley.

It was named Pig Valley because no one had wanted smelly swill troughs or cackling hens in the middle of town, so the men had cleared an out-of-the way spot partway up the slope. They'd built a pigsty, a chicken coop and a caretaker's shack.

Next to the pigsty was a small barn. Pit ponies that had been injured in the mines or needed special care were moved from the big barn in town to be nursed back to health. By Crazy Louie.

Surely a man who looked after animals couldn't be all bad?

Patrick O'Hanlan, the stable master in charge of the town barn, had always been kind to Maggie when she and Pa had paid the occasional Saturday visit. A few times he'd even let her brush the shaggy-haired ponies. Maybe Louie was like Mr. O'Hanlan, who treated all the animals in his care as if they were his very own children.

She'd never been allowed to visit the underground barn though. Deep inside Number Five Mine, the barn housed about forty horses that rarely got to see the light of day. "That's so cruel!" Maggie had cried when Pa had first told her about the ponies who lived most of the year in darkness. He didn't seem to think so, but maybe it was because he was used to the damp and the gloom and the thick black dust that choked your lungs. Not to mention the deafening roar of the hammer-drills.

Shading her eyes, Maggie stared at the farmyard. Except for a few chickens scratching in the dirt, there was no one in sight. But Louie had to be around some-where. She'd once heard Mr. Nickerson telling Pa how the only thing that could lure Louie out of the valley was a late-night poker game.

She started walking slowly along the trail that hugged the edge of the cliff. A few hundred feet over, it joined up with a wider curving trail that led down to Pig Valley.

Lucky trotted after her.

Suddenly, loud crashing sounds erupted from the forest, followed by whoops of laughter. She whirled to face the noise.

Jock burst into the clearing, followed by Davy. They were both waving long pointed sticks as if they were swords.

Chapter Nine

Jock and Davy stopped dead in their tracks, staring at Maggie. Jock's mouth snapped shut and his eyes narrowed to slits.

Maggie stared back at them, her heart sinking. Why on earth did *they* have to show up?

"Well, well," Jock said, "look who's here." Still brandishing his stick like a weapon, he started swaggering toward her.

Maggie's throat tightened. Here she was, all alone in the middle of nowhere, with no escape route in sight. And the last time she'd had a run-in with Jock, she'd left him with a fat ear. Every inch of her brain was screaming *Run*! but she wasn't about to give Jock Webster that satisfaction. Forcing herself not to hurry, she started walking slowly along the path that skirted the cliff.

"Where're you going?" Jock called.

Maggie kept walking. From behind came the sound of footsteps crashing through the underbrush. Growing louder and louder.

"What's the matter, Sullivan?" Davy jeered. "Feeling a little chicken? Cluck-cluck-cluck!"

Jock's snort of laughter sounded right behind her. Maggie stopped abruptly and whirled to face him. "I'm not afraid of *you*," she said as scornfully as she could manage. "I'm going somewhere."

"Going somewhere?" Jock repeated, his eyebrows lifting. "The only thing around here is—" His voice cut off, and then it rose in disbelief. "You going to see Crazy Louie?"

"None of your business!" Maggie snapped.

"You are," he crowed. "So is he your *boyfriend* or something? You *crazy* about each other?" He hooted at his own wit.

Davy snickered and tapped Jock's arm with the end of his stick. "Hey, why doesn't she ask him about the dead man?"

The *dead* man? What was he talking about? Maggie tried desperately to keep her face blank.

Davy nodded. "That's right, the dead man." He smirked at Jock, who smirked back. "Some guy who came up from Haynesville that time when the poker pot got up to five hundred. And they got into a fight and he called Louie a freak and—"

"Louie pulled a knife." Jock's voice drowned out Davy's. "Then he dragged the guy outside. And then the guy just *disappeared*. I heard he's buried right down there." He pointed into the valley with his stick.

"You're just making that up," Maggie said hotly. Trying to scare me, she said to herself. Of course she didn't believe one single word of it. But somehow a chill was snaking its way down her spine.

"Oh yeah?" Jock took a step forward. Suddenly he was so close that she could see tiny freckles on his cheeks and the faint shadow of hairs growing above his lip. "Why don't you ask him then?" he said with a challenging look.

Maggie's whole body had started to tremble, but she wasn't going to let these creeps see any hint of fear. She crossed her arms over her chest. "Why should I?" she said scornfully to Jock. "Everyone knows you're a big fat liar."

Jock's face flushed crimson. "Oh yeah?" he snarled and lifted his stick.

Lucky growled deep in his throat.

"Shut up, you stupid mutt!" The stick rose, and then it smacked down hard on Lucky's back.

Maggie watched in horror as Lucky toppled over the edge of the cliff.

Chapter Ten

"Lucky!" she screeched. Without even stopping to think, Maggie leapt after him. *Oooof*! She landed with a thud and toppled forward on hands and knees, her chin grazing a clump of larkspur. Hastily she scrambled to her feet.

Where was Lucky? She took one step, then another.

Suddenly she was tumbling down the slope like a boulder in a landslide. Bushes clawed at her arms and legs. Dirt burrowed into her mouth. A fiery pain seared her back.

Owww! Her head!

Everything went black.

Eww, what was that? Something tugging at her face. Something *wet*? She opened her eyes.

A hot rough tongue swiped frantically across her cheek.

"Lucky," she whispered. She lifted her head. Owww!! Pain stabbed like a spike, and a dark mist swirled in front of her eyes. Her head thudded into the dirt.

Lucky pawed at her chest, barking wildly.

Even the tiniest movement hurt so much. "Stop... sit," she hissed.

Lucky sank obediently to the ground. Plopping his chin on her chest, he heaved a long snuffly sigh. For a long moment Maggie lay there, listening to him breathe. His comforting doggy scent flowed into her nostrils. There were other smells too—cedar, earth, crushed fern.

She lifted a hand as heavy as a rock and let it fall onto his fur. She opened her eyes again.

A big brown eye was staring right into hers.

Maggie smiled and shifted her head slightly. The pain seemed to radiate from a single spot above and behind her right temple. She touched it.

Wet. And sticky.

Her fingers were coated with blood! A shiver skittered from her head to her toes, and her head started to spin. "Help," she moaned.

Lucky raised his head.

"Lucky...up...get...Mama."

Lucky scrambled to his feet and stood without moving, gazing down at her. Either he wasn't sure what to do or he didn't want to leave her.

She pointed a trembling finger. "Go. Home."

Lucky trotted a few feet away; then he stopped and whined, peering anxiously back at her.

"Go!" she said, making a shooing motion. Pain jolted through her head and she closed her eyes. As if from a great distance she heard a yelp, followed by crashing sounds.

Then there was only silence.

What was that? Maggie's eyes flew open and she found herself staring up at a cedar branch. From somewhere high above her, a raven cawed angrily. What was happening? Where was she?

A volley of barking answered the raven's cry.

Lucky! The cliff! Falling! Memories came flooding back.

The barking grew louder, more frenzied.

"Hold on, I'm coming," said a gravelly voice.

That wasn't Mama's voice!

A second later Lucky scrambled up the slope,

followed by a savage-looking stranger. A man with masses of tangled black hair that sprang wildly from his head and tumbled halfway to his shoulders. His face was hidden behind a shaggy black beard.

It had to be Crazy Louie!

Chapter Eleven

The man scowled down at her. It was an eerie, inhuman scowl. One eye squinted, but the other seemed frozen in place. An icy black marble of an eye. What was wrong with him? Maggie's heart hammered in her chest.

What if he thought she was trespassing? What was he going to *do* to her?

What about the dead man?

She had to get away from him! Wincing at the pain, she struggled up onto her elbows. And was almost knocked down again by Lucky. He pawed at her stomach, whining furiously. Then he turned to bark at the stranger. The man's finger shot out. "Sit!"

Lucky dropped to the ground as if he'd been smacked. His jaw clamped shut.

The man stepped closer to Maggie, and then he crouched beside her. A stench like rotting manure filled her nostrils. And a whiff of something else—dead fish? Overlying it all was the telltale scent of a heavy smoker.

She gaped up at him. Starting at the edge of the frozen eye, a puckered red scar zigzagged down his cheek and vanished into his beard.

"…get up."

Only one side of his mouth was moving! Maggie's left elbow gave way and she thudded onto the dirt.

"I *said*, can you get up?"

"It hurts," she whispered. "My head and my back."

The man's scowl deepened. "Well, you can't stay here."

What did he want her to do? How was she going to get out of here? If only Mama would come. Her lips trembled.

Suddenly he bent forward, thrust his arms under her body and lurched to his feet. For a split second Maggie lay stunned in his arms. Then she started wriggling like a hooked fish.

"Cut it out," he barked.

She froze.

He shifted position, squeezed her even tighter

and started staggering down the hill. Lucky trotted alongside.

With every step, Maggie's head throbbed, and she felt as if she were about to throw up. Where was he taking her? A few minutes later she found out. Breathing so heavily that he grunted with every step, the man stumbled across the farmyard toward a wooden shack that was half the size of her house. He kicked open the door and headed for a narrow bed that was shoved into a corner of the room.

Without a word, he lowered her onto the faded brown quilt. Then he strode across the room to a sink and turned on the tap.

Maggie watched him, torn between exhaustion, fear and a growing sense of relief. Surely he wouldn't have brought her here if he was planning to kill her?

The bed shuddered and Lucky landed in a heap by her side. He licked her cheek and flopped down with his back nestled against her and his three legs sticking out into the room. A deep sigh rumbled from his throat.

For the first time since she'd opened her eyes at the bottom of the cliff, Maggie felt her body relax. Lucky was acting as naturally as if he were stretched out on his own back porch. But what would Louie do when he spotted a dog lying on his bed? Before she could act, he came tromping across the floor carrying a wet cloth.

He gazed down at Lucky, and the corner of his mouth twitched.

Was he *smiling*?

"What's his name?" said the gravelly voice.

"Lucky."

"Smart mutt." Suddenly he leaned forward and his shaggy head loomed above hers. He swiped at her temple with the cloth.

It felt as if she'd been smacked by an icy snowball. "Owwww!" she gasped.

"What are you doing?" cried Mama as she rushed into the room with Elly and Jock at her heels.

Chapter Twelve

The room exploded into motion. Lucky leapt off the bed, barking wildly. Louie dropped the cloth and lunged across the room. As if by magic, a shotgun appeared in his hands.

"Mama!" Maggie cried.

"Maggie!" Mama whooshed toward the bed like a tornado. She turned to face Louie, flinging her arms out to the sides.

The gun was pointing straight at Mama! Maggie grabbed the back of Mama's skirt and tugged hard, trying to pull her down on the bed. Lucky's bark turned into an earsplitting howl. "Quiet," Louie ordered.

Lucky shut up instantly. Everyone else froze.

Then Mama held out her hand, palm facing up as if she were begging for coins. "Please," she said in a low voice, "put that thing down."

For an endless moment Louie scowled ferociously at Mama. Then, slowly, he lowered the gun. He clomped over to the table that stood in the middle of the room and yanked with his foot at one of the hard-backed chairs. Laying the gun on the table, he sat down heavily.

Mama turned to Maggie. "Are you all right?" she demanded. "What *happened*?"

Maggie had never been so glad to see her mother. More than anything in the world, she wanted to bury her head in Mama's lap and burst into tears. But how could she, with everyone watching? She sucked in a deep, shuddery breath. "I…he…"

"Did he hurt you?" Mama said fiercely.

"No." Maggie shook her head. "He *helped* me." She clutched Mama's arm. "My head hurts," she wailed.

Ten minutes later her bones had been checked, her wounds cleaned and dressed, and she was half sitting, squished cozily between Mama and Lucky. The sharp pain in her head had shrunk to a dull throb.

"Here," Mama said to Elly, handing her the cloth and the bowl of water she'd been using. "Wash this out at the sink, please." She stood up, walked over to the door and opened it. "We're finished," she called.

Louie followed her into the room, a cigarette pinched between the thumb and forefinger of his right hand.

Jock appeared in the doorway behind him. He stared across the room at Maggie but didn't step inside.

Maggie stared back at him, trying to decipher the look on his face.

"Mr....Jenkins, is it?" Mama said.

Louie nodded and dragged heavily on his cigarette. Lifting his chin, he blew a stream of smoke toward the ceiling.

Maggie blinked. Would Mama say anything? She hated cigars and cigarettes with a passion. Of course, it wasn't *her* house Louie was smoking in.

Mama raised a hand to her mouth, coughed delicately and said, "I must apologize for rushing into your home the way I did. My daughter has explained to me how you helped her." She held out her hand. "I owe you my thanks."

Louie stared at the hand as if he thought it might slap him. A red stain flooded his forehead and the portion of his cheeks that wasn't hidden by his beard. He cleared his throat as if to speak, but no words came out. Instead he jammed the cigarette between his lips and brushed Mama's fingers for the tiniest instant. After taking another deep drag on the cigarette, he cleared his throat again. "About the gun," he began.

Mama held up a hand to stop him. "Please, don't worry," she said quietly. "Anyone would be wary of strangers bursting into their home." Her face changed, as if she had suddenly remembered something. She looked at Maggie, then over at Jock, then back at Maggie again.

Maggie's throat tightened. She knew that look.

"Now. I would like to find out exactly what happened on that cliff," Mama said in her steeliest voice. "Jock said that you fell?"

Jock said? Now that she had time to think, Maggie found herself brimming with questions. What exactly *had* happened? Jock had obviously gone to fetch Mama. But *why*? And where was Davy?

She looked at Jock, who was still staring at her. What *was* that look in his eyes? Was he trying to say he was sorry?

"It was an accident," she said and noted the look of relief that flashed across Jock's face. She rushed on. "We were walking along the cliff and Lucky fell, and then I went after him, and then I fell, and then I sent Lucky for help."

"But what were you doing up there in the first place?" Mama said.

For a moment there was silence, broken only by the tick-tick-tick of a clock.

"I was coming to see him." Maggie pointed at Louie. "Mr. Winters told me to."

"*Mr. Winters* told you to?" Mama repeated, her eyebrows lifting.

"Uh-huh. He said I should ask him to take Lucky." She looked beseechingly at Mama. "Do I have to?"

Louie made a strange growling noise, thrust past Mama and stepped toward the bed.

Chapter Thirteen

The sun beat down hard on Maggie's head as she trudged along the road. Lucky, trotting ahead, kicked up wispy dust devils with every step. Even the weeds drooped, as if they couldn't be bothered to hold their stems straight. She couldn't remember the last time it had rained.

Lucky's back stiffened and he started to bark. Two ponies grazing in the paddock raised their heads in alarm. Fortunately they were separated from Lucky by a sturdy wood-and-wire fence.

"Stop it, silly. They're just ponies."

Lucky shook his head and let out a giant sneeze. The gray pony cantered a few steps farther away.

"Bless you," Maggie said.

The ponies stared at Lucky for a moment longer and lowered their heads. Both the gray and the chestnut looked sleek and well-fed. Had Louie nursed them back to health?

An image of his face—that scar, that eye—floated eerily through her head. What was she doing here anyway? If it hadn't been for Mama…She glared at the paddock. Somewhere deep inside, though, a voice was telling her that Mama was right. What other choice did she have? So she'd finally agreed to Mama's plan for Lucky to spend some time at Louie's farm.

Louie, who seemed to have taken to Mama, had agreed too. After Mama had calmed him down and talked his ear off. Of course Mama was good at talking people into doing things they didn't really want to do.

She looked at Lucky, who had stopped to sniff at a freshly dug hole by the side of the trail. What if he hated the farm? Or—suddenly a sharp pain knifed at her chest—what if he loved it?

How could she give him up?

But the days till they had to leave were flying by faster than a flock of Canada geese. If only she could freeze this exact slice of time. Or, better still, turn back the clock. Back to the day before Number Three Mine had collapsed in a heap, burying Pa and two other miners under a shroud of granite and coal.

Buried. Gone. Forever.

The one person who had understood her better than anyone else in the whole entire world.

The chestnut let out a shrill whinny, and both ponies exploded into motion.

Startled, Maggie froze for an instant; then she looked to see what had spooked them.

Louie was stumping toward the paddock, a handful of carrots dangling from his hand.

Maggie's heart fluttered. He sure didn't look civilized, despite what Mama thought. "What an odd character," she'd said as they walked slowly home from the farm. "He looks like the roughest old tramp, but he appears to be a civilized man." That was high praise coming from Mama. Of course he *had* just agreed to do exactly what she wanted. And he *had* rescued her daughter.

But Mama didn't know about the dead man.

Should she have told her? Or let Elly come along today like Mama had wanted? No! Maggie lifted her chin. Jock and Davy were just lying through their teeth, and she wasn't the least bit afraid of Louie Jenkins. Besides, who needed Elly sticking her nose in where it didn't belong?

She took a deep breath and marched toward the paddock. Lucky bounded ahead of her, making a beeline for the fence. He stuck his nose through the wire mesh as far as it would go and gazed intently at the ponies.

Maggie swallowed hard. "Hello."

Louie didn't reply, just stared at her with that freakish half-scowl. No doubt feeling mad that he'd ever let Mama talk him into this. Maybe he didn't want Lucky after all. Maybe they should just leave.

"What happened to his leg?" Louie growled, nodding his head in Lucky's direction. The tangled locks of his hair quivered like a nest of black snakes.

Maggie almost leapt backward, but she caught herself just in time. "Cougar trap," she said breathlessly. "Pa rescued him and then gave him to me."

Louie grunted and thrust the carrots in her direction. "Here. You feed Smoky 'n' Belle while he and I get acquainted."

Without even realizing how it had happened, Maggie found herself clutching the feathery green stems. It was the scar that kept stealing her attention. The scar and the eye. She just couldn't seem to stop staring. And wondering.

The words came tumbling out of her mouth. "What happened to your face?"

A dark tide of crimson swept across Louie's forehead and cheeks and vanished into his beard.

He leaned menacingly toward her.

Chapter Fourteen

Why on earth had she opened her big mouth? Maggie stumbled backward and turned to flee, still clutching the carrots. Lucky bounded to her side.

Suddenly, from behind, came an odd sound—half snarl, half bark. What was that?! She paused in mid-stride and peered over her shoulder. Louie's mouth was oddly twisted—one side curved up instead of down. Was he…laughing?

"I don't bite, y' know," he said. "Maybe bark a little." He made the funny sound again. "You better come on back."

Slowly Maggie turned to face him.

Louie scratched his beard. "Got kicked by a horse a long time ago. My fault, not his. Me being young and stupid."

Maggie tried to picture a younger Louie, without the puckered scar and the frozen eye. Could he have been handsome? While she stared, Louie was fumbling in his pocket. He pulled out a grimy white cloth and unwrapped it. Inside lay a chunk of hard yellow cheese.

Lucky's nose lifted. He trotted forward.

Louie broke off a corner and held it out to Lucky, who wolfed it down without even a backward glance at Maggie. When he whined eagerly for more, Louie gave him a second piece and rubbed the top of his head.

"How did you know he loves cheese?" Maggie said wonderingly.

Louie shrugged. "Had a mutt that was crazy about it."

"You did?" Maggie's eyebrows rose. "What happened to him?"

The corner of his mouth tightened. "Dead."

Dead? Maggie's heart skipped a beat. Dead like… Don't be stupid, she scolded herself. Jock and Davy were just trying to spook you. But what had happened to the dog? A picture formed in her head. A shaggy white shape cowering in the dirt, Louie aiming the shotgun.

"Made it to fifteen, though. A good long life."

The image vanished. See, Maggie jeered at herself silently, the dog died of old age. She gazed at Lucky, who was waiting hopefully for another hunk of cheese. Would he live to be fifteen? Would she even know? Tears pricked at her eyelids.

The chestnut let out another shrill whinny.

Lucky barked, but his gaze didn't shift from the cheese.

"It's coming," Louie called. He looked at Maggie. "She's waiting for her carrots," he said, pointing a thumb at the paddock. "Go on, feed her and Smoky, and I'll take Lucky to the farm. Come to the barn when you're done."

The more he spoke, the more she found herself getting used to the way his face moved. Or didn't move. Still, it wasn't surprising that he'd chosen to hide from the world.

Maggie blinked. Wait a minute, what had he just said? He was taking Lucky to the farm? Without her? Ha! Not in a million years would Lucky ever go off like that, not unless she told him to.

"C'mon, boy," Louie called, jiggling the cloth that held the cheese. He turned and started tramping toward the farmyard.

After a quick, almost furtive, glance at Maggie, Lucky galloped after him.

Her jaw dropped. That sneaky rat! He was deserting her? For a savage with a hunk of cheese? She didn't know whether to laugh, cry or kick the nearest fencepost.

Ten minutes later she was jogging toward the barn. On any other day she would have loved feeding Smoky and Belle, but today she'd rushed through it as if it had been one of her kitchen chores.

A sudden breeze puffed at her face, carrying with it the pungent aroma of hay and manure. It smelled a lot like Louie. Just beyond the barn, in a fenced area attached to the pigsty, several grayish pink pigs lay stretched in the dirt.

"Yeowwwwwllllll!"

Lucky streaked out of the barn with his tail tucked between his legs. Streaking right behind him was an enormous gray tabby cat!

Lucky charged straight at Maggie, skidded around behind her and buried his head in her skirt.

The cat stopped a few feet away. It arched its back, scowled ferociously at Lucky and let out a sizzling hiss. It looked like an angry raccoon.

"Fierce, ain't she?" Louie appeared in the barn doorway, carrying a broom and a silver pail. He set the pail down in the dirt and leaned the broom against the wall of the barn.

Lucky's muzzle peeked around the side of Maggie's skirt. He rubbed his head against her thigh and whimpered softly.

"Hmph." Maggie frowned down at him. "*Now* you want me, when there's a big mean cat after you." She looked at the cat, which had relaxed and was now calmly licking its front paw. "How come she was chasing Lucky?"

"He stumbled on her and her kittens." He walked over to the cat and knelt to rub it behind the ears. "You sure scared the bejeebers out of him, didn't you, Sadie?" He made the funny barking sound again.

On any other day, Maggie would have been thrilled to bits at the very mention of kittens. But right now she couldn't have cared less if he'd said they were fuzzy white polar bear cubs.

She was watching Sadie.

The cat had nestled her head into Louie's hand, accepting his attentions like a queen. Maggie heard a low rumbling purr. They looked so happy. A fierce pain shot through her head and came to rest at the spot where she'd banged it. "We have to go now," she said abruptly.

Louie squinted up at her. "They better make friends first." He looked at Lucky and patted the ground with his fingers. "C'mon, Lucky. Come and meet Sadie."

As if he were spellbound, Lucky crept forward a few paces and stopped.

"Good boy." Louie rubbed Sadie's head again. "Now you be nice," he said to her. He stretched his free hand out to Lucky. "C'mon, she won't hurt you."

Slowly Lucky walked forward and sniffed Louie's hand. Then he bent his head and sniffed at Sadie.

Sadie's eyes narrowed to slits, but she didn't move. Or hiss.

Lucky sank down on his haunches beside her and rested his head on Louie's knee.

"See? Everything's gonna be fine," Louie said, squinting up at Maggie.

How could he say that? Everything wasn't going to be fine! Maggie stared at him, overcome by a feeling of helplessness that quickly turned to anger. "No, it isn't!" she cried. "I hate you and I hate Lucky too!" She hurtled blindly across the farmyard, heading for the trail.

Chapter Fifteen

Maggie charged pell-mell along the path, blinking back the tears that kept threatening to fall. Clouds of dust swirled around her feet, making it seem as if she were cloaked in a thick gray fog. Faint sounds of barking and shouting floated through the air.

She didn't stop, didn't even pause. Let Lucky stay here if he loved it so much. She was going home!

Lucky charged up beside her, barking and peering at her with worried brown eyes.

"Go away!"

Footsteps pounded behind her, followed by loud gasping breaths. "Wait," Louie called.

Maggie tried desperately to speed up, but it was no use. Her legs felt like cooked noodles and her throat burned all the way down to her chest.

"Will you stop, for jiminy's sake?"

Maggie peered over her shoulder. Louie's face was as red as the lipstick Mama used to wear when she and Pa went dancing at the Saturday night socials. There was no way he could catch her if she just kept moving.

Her toe struck something hard and she tumbled to the ground. Lucky nudged in close, his wet nose butting against her cheek. "Stop it," she said, thrusting his head away.

He whined softly.

"You okay?" Louie's gasps turned into a deep hacking cough.

Maggie scrambled to her feet, wiping her hands on her dress. Both knees were filthy and the left one hurt. She took a wobbly step; then she started to walk away.

Louie's cough sputtered and died. "Will you stop acting so goldarn pig-headed?"

"At least *I'm* not crazy," Maggie muttered under her breath.

"What?"

Had he heard? A hot wave of shame washed over her face and neck. She'd sounded every bit as mean as Jock and Davy. Louie might be strange, but he had a good reason for it. And it didn't make him crazy. "Nothing," she said.

Louie cleared his throat. "Look, you got every right to be mad."

Maggie took one more step. Then she stopped. Her knee throbbed painfully.

"I'd be madder 'n heck too."

Maggie half turned to face him.

He was fumbling in his shirt pocket. He pulled out the familiar red and gold pack, lit a cigarette and took a deep drag. Which set off another coughing fit. When it finally died away, he pointed the cigarette at Lucky. "Don't you be mad at him, though. He's just doing what he's got to do."

Maggie glanced at Lucky, who was sniffing warily at a clump of foul-smelling chocolate lilies; then she shot a puzzled look at Louie. "What?"

"He knows, that's what." Louie nodded his head in Lucky's direction. "I've seen it over and over. Animals know things." He picked a speck of tobacco off his lower lip. "He's doing what he's got to do," he repeated.

"What are you talking about?" she snapped, not even caring if she sounded rude. She was in no mood to be confused.

"He's trying to move on. The best he can."

"I don't believe it!" Maggie glared at Louie. "Lucky doesn't *want* to move on." Her heart was pounding like a hammer banging in a nail. There was no way that Lucky wanted to move on without her. He just *couldn't*, any more than she could.

Louie shrugged. "When you've worked with animals as long as I have…" His voice trailed off and they both gazed at Lucky. By now his snout was buried deep in the dirt and his tail was wagging a mile a minute. Probably scaring the daylights out of some poor field mouse.

He looked as if he didn't have a care in the world.

"Lucky!" Maggie shouted.

Lucky raised his head and peered over his shoulder. If she hadn't been so furious, she might even have laughed. He looked as if he'd stuck his head into a bowl of chocolate pudding. Shaking his head wildly, he let loose with a gigantic sneeze. Bits of dirt flew everywhere.

"Come!" Maggie called out.

He trotted obediently to her side, and she turned to leave.

"See you soon, I guess," Louie said.

Maggie walked off without answering. But inside a voice was nattering, *You didn't have to be so rude. It's not as if any of this is his fault.* She heaved a deep sigh. If only things could go back to the way they used to be.

By the time they rounded the corner of the house twenty minutes later, Maggie's whole leg was throbbing and she felt as if she were running a fever. Lucky streaked for the water pail that she kept for him in a shady spot at the foot of the back stairs. He started slurping noisily.

Usually Maggie plunked down on the bottom step to keep him company while he drank, but today she tramped up the stairs to the porch. She sank down on the old wicker rocker and closed her eyes. The last wisp of breeze had died and the heat felt like a too-heavy quilt.

Lucky padded up the stairs and flopped down on her feet.

She scooted them out of the way as if they'd been scalded. "Go," she said, pointing to the other end of the porch. "You're too hot." She planted a foot on each of the chair runners, out of Lucky's reach.

He flashed her a reproachful look, wiggled himself backward a few inches and rested his head on his paws. A lingering sigh wheezed from his throat and faded sadly away.

The voice nattered again, *How can you be so mean to him*? But look what he did to me, she argued silently, cozying up to Louie and leaving me behind. She frowned down at Lucky's head.

The screen door creaked open and Mama stepped out. For once she wasn't wearing an apron over her crisp yellow dress. "I thought I heard you out here. How did it go?"

Maggie shrugged.

Mama laid a gentle hand on Maggie's hair. "I know it's difficult, but I'm sure Mr. Jenkins was—" Mama's voice broke off, and then it rose sharply. "What happened to your dress? And your knees?" Her fingers slid under Maggie's chin and lifted it. "Did something happen? I knew I should have made Elly go with you."

Maggie jerked her head away. "Nothing happened. I tripped, that's all." Her voice sank to a mutter. "Everything went fine. Lucky loves it there."

"Oh." Mama went quiet for a moment. "Well, that's what we wanted, isn't it?" she said in a false cheery tone that Maggie hated. "I'm just so pleased that we've found a good solution."

And that's all Lucky is to you, isn't he? thought Maggie. Just another problem to be solved. All of a sudden her head felt as if it were about to explode. Scrambling to her feet, she scowled at Mama. "It's too hot. I'm going to the river."

Mama's lips tightened. But when she spoke, her voice was calm. "That's a good idea. Why don't you take some bread and cheese with you? And there's fresh lemonade."

A few minutes later Maggie banged out onto the porch. She was carrying her school lunch pail, a screw-top jar filled with lemonade and an old green towel. She moved toward the steps.

Lucky lifted his head and gave an enormous yawn. Then he struggled to his feet and padded after her. He sniffed at the lunch pail.

Maggie pushed his head away. "No," she said sternly. "Sit! Stay!"

Hurt brown eyes gazed up at her. Maggie shook her head. "We have to learn to get along without each other." Tears welled in her eyes and she stumbled blindly down the stairs. "Stay there," she called without turning around.

An eerie, mournful sound—part wail, part howl—rang out behind her, but Lucky didn't follow.

For the first time since she could remember, she was going to the river alone.

Chapter Sixteen

Maggie burst out of the forest into the sunshine, her breath coming in ragged gasps. She gazed down at the river. Despite having shrunk from lack of rain, it looked cool and inviting. Water droplets sparkled like diamonds as they splashed against the rocks.

There were no diamonds in the river, but there *was* gold. Years ago, Pa had told her, a prospector had found a nugget the size of his fist, and since then many smaller nuggets had been discovered. Maggie and Abigail had searched a couple of times, but neither of them had found anything.

She dropped her towel onto the rocks and placed her lunch pail and jar carefully in a clump of soft grass. Then she scuffed off her shoes and yanked her dress over her head. Thank goodness there was no one around to see her swimsuit, an Elly hand-me-down that had stretched out and faded to a whitish blue.

She picked her way gingerly down the bank until she reached the smooth gray boulder that she called Seal Rock. She sat down and dipped her big toe into the water. Oooh! It was amazingly, icily cold. Taking a deep breath, she slid both feet into the water and stood up.

The shock raced up her legs to her knees and died away as her skin went numb. Slowly she moved forward, peering down into the clear green water. She'd learned the hard way to pay close attention to her feet.

A family of ravens exploded from the treetops and winged high into the air. What had startled them? Had Lucky followed her?

No, it was a deer! A fawn, still coated in its white spots. And there was its mother. They stared solemnly at Maggie with enormous dark eyes.

She stared back, enchanted. When Lucky was around, it was a sight she never got to see.

Suddenly a rock shifted beneath her and her foot slipped. She tumbled backward, hands flying out behind her as she tried desperately to break her fall.

Bottom and hands smacked against something hard. Icy water splashed over her chin. Her right hand skidded sideways, and she clutched frantically at a clump of small stones.

Water swept into her mouth and nose. Coughing and spluttering, she clambered to her feet and staggered back to Seal Rock, still clutching the stones. She raised her hand to dump them into the river when she spotted a flash of gold. Her jaw dropped.

A nugget the size of a marble lay in the palm of her hand! It had to be worth a small fortune, maybe even fifty dollars. A vision swam into her head: A row of grand houses on an elegant tree-lined street. Maggie and Mama and Elly taking tea on the front porch of the grandest house of all.

A voice in her head pierced the vision like a darning needle pricking her finger. *Don't be ridiculous, Maggie. Even if it was worth fifty dollars, that would barely pay for a month's rent. Besides, you must save it for your education.* It was as if Mama were perched right beside her on the rock.

Maggie shook her head and flung the other stones into the river. She gazed down at the nugget. Her nugget. It was amazingly beautiful—a bright yellow gold. And worth more money than she'd ever seen in her life. Was there some way she could use it to help Lucky? What if she took him to Vancouver, paid for him to stay somewhere close to the boarding house? Went to visit him every day? She tried to picture Lucky trotting along a noisy car-filled street. Strangers gawking at his missing leg. Would she have to drag him along with a leash?

Other pictures floated through her head. Lucky with his head raised, sniffing at the mountain breeze. Bounding eagerly toward Smoky and Belle. Lying on his belly in the sunshine, watching the chickens and the pigs. He looked so happy. As if he was right where he belonged.

She heaved a deep sigh. Lucky had never known anything but the mountain. How could he be happy living in a city? Especially when he could be living on a farm. And what about Mama? She'd never let Maggie bring him, not in a million years.

She sighed again and stroked the nugget with her finger. At least one good thing had happened. The nugget was hers, not anyone else's. And it was going to stay hers until *she* was ready to use it.

After gobbling her bread and cheese and gulping the warm lemonade, she sprinted along the trail toward home. She bounded up the front porch steps and into the house. "I'm just going to change," she called to Mama in the kitchen. Carefully shutting the bedroom door, she headed straight for the trunk of clothes she and Mama had packed.

At the very bottom of the trunk, underneath her winter coat, lay Pa's old brown leather jacket. Already tucked inside it was a small wooden bear Pa had carved for her one winter, along with a black and white eagle feather that she and Pa had found, and a funny poem Pa had written called "Zig-Zaggy Maggie."

She slid the nugget deep into one of the jacket pockets, covered it up again and closed the lid. Then she put on her green dress and headed for the kitchen. Mama and Elly were drinking their afternoon cup of tea, which Maggie always thought was a strange thing to do on a hot day.

"How was the river?" Mama said.

"Good." Maggie opened the back door and peered out. "Where's Lucky?"

"Wasn't he with you?" Mama sipped daintily at her tea.

"No." Maggie yanked the door wide and stepped onto the porch. "Lucky," she called.

There was no welcoming woof, no scramble of paws on the stairs. Just silence.

"Lucky! Come here, boy!"

Her heart started to pound. Lucky hadn't gone off by himself for months and months. Where was he? Had he followed her to the river after all? Fallen in somewhere?

Had he tangled with a cougar?

Chapter Seventeen

"Lucky! Lucky!" Maggie circled the house, calling frantically. But all she saw was his much-chewed red ball, abandoned beneath an alder tree, and an old hambone, poking out of his favorite burying spot.

"He can't have gone far," Mama said from the porch. "I'm sure he'll be back."

Her words were drowned out by the thoughts hammering inside Maggie's skull. This is all your fault, she thought. You shouldn't have been so mean to him. You should have let him come with you. "I'm going back to the river!" she cried, sprinting for the trail. "Lucky," she kept yelling as she raced along, "here, Lucky!"

When she reached the water she plunged in, not even stopping to remove her shoes. She waded past Seal Rock to the high jagged boulder that commanded a view of the river. Climbing as high as she could, she searched in every direction.

Nothing. Nothing but stupid water and stupid trees and a pair of red-tailed hawks soaring overhead. If only she could fly too, just swoop down on Lucky from the sky!

Where was he? Think, she told herself fiercely, where would he go if he couldn't be with me?

Twenty minutes later she charged into the Pig Valley farmyard, puffing like a steam engine. "Lucky!" she shouted.

Chickens scattered in all directions, clucking in alarm, and the pigs raised their dozy heads. But no dog came running.

"What the heck! What's all the ruckus?" Louie demanded, stepping out of the barn. A cigarette dangled from his mouth, and he was wiping his hands on a greasy rag.

"Where's Lucky?" Maggie cried.

Louie stuffed the rag into his back pocket and shook his head. "Not here. Why, what's happened?"

"I thought…" Maggie's face crumpled. "I have to go!" Whirling, she started to race away.

"Hey, hold on a minute."

She didn't have time to hold on! But she stopped

anyway, impatience vibrating through every fiber of her body. "I can't. Lucky ran away and it's all my fault!"

Louie tossed the cigarette butt onto the dirt and crushed it with his boot. "Well, I don't know what happened, but I know this: he'll be fine. He's smart and he's tough."

"But I was *horrible* to him." Maggie's chin wobbled and she bit down hard on her lip.

Louie scratched his beard. "Did you kick him? Give him a slap, maybe?"

"No!" Maggie glared at Louie, her tears forgotten. "I would *never* hurt Lucky."

Louie's hand shot up like a stop sign. "Calm down. I believe you. But just remember that a dog'll forgive and forget," he snapped his fingers, "just like that. I bet you anything he's already home."

"You think so?" Maggie's face brightened as she grasped at this straw of hope. Louie knew animals, didn't he? Not like Mama.

He nodded. "Tell you what, though, I'll take a look around here. If he shows up, I'll bring him to your place. One over from Marshall's, right?"

Louie would leave Pig Valley? For her? When she'd been almost as horrible to him as she'd been to Lucky? The way she'd been acting, it was a lot better than she deserved. She nodded. "It's the second, turning off Logan's Trail. I...thank you." She flashed him a grateful half smile, and then she turned and started jogging across the yard. Her shins ached and a blister oozed on her right heel, but she wasn't going to let anything slow her down.

Not if Lucky was waiting at home.

By the time she reached the last stretch of the journey, her jog had slowed to a limping walk. Her shoe rubbed painfully against the raw patch with every step. Her throat felt as if it had been scraped with sandpaper.

Shrill yelps ripped through the air from somewhere in front of her.

Was that Lucky? It had to be! The noise was coming from up ahead, past that bend in the trail. If only she could see through the bushes. She rushed forward.

The yelping turned into a frantic high-pitched yowl. "Lucky!" She hurtled around the bend.

And stopped, her jaw dropping in shock. There he was, a rope tied around his neck, being dragged along the trail by Jock Webster!

Chapter Eighteen

Jock stopped too and gaped back at her. His shirt was half pulled out of his jeans, and there were large dirt smears on both knees. Lucky strained against the rope collar, barking hysterically.

"Let him go!" Maggie screeched. She charged forward along the path, her hands clenching into fists.

"I wasn't doing anything," he yelled, flinging the end of the rope at her as if it had burst into flames. "*Here.*"

Lucky flew like a cannonball, knocking her backward onto the dirt. Welcoming yips burst from his throat and he washed her face with slobbery kisses.

Maggie wrapped her arms around his neck and breathed in his smell. "I'm sorry," she whispered. "I'm so sorry."

Suddenly a shadow loomed above their heads. Maggie's stomach muscles clenched. "That's enough, boy," she said to Lucky and wiggled out from under his body. She pushed herself onto her knees and peered up at Jock. "What were you doing to him?" she demanded.

He scowled. "Gimme my rope back."

Move back then, she wanted to snap, and stop crowding me. But instead she fumbled for the loop of rope that encircled Lucky's neck. Strange, it wasn't tight at all. So Jock hadn't been trying to strangle him. But what had he been doing? Or planning to do?

She finally managed to undo the knot and thrust the rope at Jock. "Here."

He grabbed it and turned to leave.

She had to know. "Wait."

He took a step, then another, and then he stopped.

"Listen," she said, trying her hardest to sound calm and reasonable. "I'd just like to know what happened, okay?"

Jock spun on his heel. "We found your stupid mutt over behind the bunkhouse."

The bunkhouse? It was on the way to the farm, sort of. Maybe Lucky *had* been trying to get to Louie. And she really couldn't blame him.

Maggie was strictly forbidden to go anywhere near the bunkhouse, but boys like Jock and Davy loved hanging around down there. During the rowdy weekend poker parties, many card players tossed their empty beer and liquor bottles out the windows for the kids to collect and cash in at the store. Sometimes the bottles landed in the dirt and sometimes they landed in the garbage heaped behind the building.

"He was nosing around in a pile of broken glass," Jock said.

Broken glass?! Horrified, Maggie examined Lucky's nose and mouth. No cuts or dried blood. Next she peered down at his paws. But there was no way he could have raced at her like that if he'd gashed a paw.

Jock was still talking. "So we got a rope and I was taking him to your place, and then you started squawking like a chicken."

"But *why*?" Maggie said, gaping at him. "You said he ought to be shot and then you pushed…" Her voice trailed off as a dark flush spread across Jock's face. She gazed at him wonderingly. He was telling the truth about rescuing Lucky, she was sure of it. But *why* had he done it?

The rope twitched in his hands.

"Never mind," she said quickly. "Thanks." Feeling her own cheeks growing hot, she glanced down at Lucky. He was sitting quietly at her side, tongue hanging out, panting gently. Jock didn't seem to bother him one little bit.

For a moment everything was silent. Then a dry twig crackled under Jock's foot. "I didn't push…I didn't mean for him to fall," he muttered. "And then *you* went charging after him like a maniac." Maggie opened her mouth indignantly, but Jock's words were hurtling at her like stones. "And then you fell, and then you were just lying there."

He glared at her as if the whole thing had been her fault.

Maggie tried not to glare back. And you just left me lying there, didn't you? she thought. Maggie sucked in a deep breath and stroked the silky fur on Lucky's head. She gave his neck a gentle squeeze and stood up. "And that's when you went to get my mother?"

Jock hesitated and gave a small tight-lipped nod. "We thought you were…" His voice trailed off.

You could have at least climbed down to check, she felt like saying, but she bit back the words. At least he'd gone to get Mama. And now this thing with Lucky. She was finding it hard to believe, but then she'd been wrong about Louie too. "I don't think Louie's so bad," she blurted out, "and I don't think he killed anybody either."

"You don't know anything about it," Jock said flatly.

"Neither do you." She and Jock traded accusing stares.

"Well, I know one thing," Jock said. "It's not normal to hole yourself up like that."

"He hates people staring at him," Maggie said hotly. "He got kicked by a horse a long time ago and it wrecked his face, that's all."

"Hmph." Jock flicked the rope savagely at a huckleberry bush. A flurry of tiny green leaves showered down.

"I like him," she declared, surprising herself as well as Jock. Mama had been right after all. Louie might look and act strange, but he was a civilized man. "And he's really good with animals." Fixing her gaze on the bush, she lowered her voice. "He's going to take Lucky when we leave."

Jock made a snorting sound. "You're giving your precious mutt to Crazy Louie?"

"Stop calling him that!" Maggie snapped back. "Lucky likes him, and he'll have a great life on the farm." As she uttered the words, it dawned on her that she really meant them.

Jock was staring at her, an odd expression flitting across his face. He looked over at Lucky, who had grown tired of sitting and was snuffling happily at a hole in the base of a cedar tree. "Maybe I'll get a dog sometime."

Maggie's mouth fell open. She had never been more astonished to hear anything in her entire life. As she watched, a tide of crimson flooded over Jock's face and neck. "One with four legs, though," he said hastily, flicking his rope at the bush again.

Maggie choked back a nasty reply. Some things would never change.

Jock was gathering in his rope as if it were the most important job in the world. "I'll keep an eye on him if you want," he said carelessly. "Just to make sure."

Maggie blinked. Had she heard right? "You mean Lucky? Keep an eye on Lucky?"

He nodded, his gaze still focused on the rope.

All kinds of feelings were jumbling around inside Maggie. Surprise, of course. But she was also feeling oddly shy. Or was it embarrassed? And mixed in with the rest was a huge dollop of curiosity. What had really made him decide to help Lucky? Was it guilt? Or something else? Whatever it was, it seemed as if he did want to help. "Okay," she said slowly. "Thanks."

"I better get going." Jock turned to leave and took a few steps forward. Suddenly he stopped and peered over his shoulder. "Good luck with everything."

And then he was gone.

For a long moment Maggie stared after him. Then she walked over to Lucky, who was pawing at a clump of dead leaves. "Well, what do you think about that?" she said softly.

Lucky peered up at her and shook his head.

She ruffled his fur. "C'mon, boy, let's go home."

Chapter Nineteen

For the last time, Maggie stood near (but not too near) the edge of the cliff, gazing down. A chilly gust of wind sent a shiver skittering along her spine. Today the sky was as gray as an old weathered barn, and the forest below had darkened almost to black.

It had been a week crammed with "last times," and she was feeling numb from too many good-bye dinners, especially the one at Abigail's. Maggie hadn't been sure that she even wanted to go to the Brysons', but Mama had told her not to be silly.

Mrs. Bryson had outdone herself with an enormous feast of roast beef and gravy, mashed potatoes, melt-in-your-mouth popovers, buttered baby carrots and about a million different kinds of desserts. She'd even given Mama her highly secret recipe for bumbleberry crumble cake.

Maggie had eaten two huge pieces, just in case Mama never got around to making any.

Besides the food, there had been one other good thing about the evening. Jessie wasn't there. For the first time in a long time it was just Maggie and Abigail. Maggie jiggled her wrist and listened to the clink-clink of the charms dangling from her bracelet. Abigail had given it to her, along with an elegant box of lavender writing paper. At that point, Abigail had burst into tears and Maggie had blinked hard, and then they'd both promised to write.

Abigail had made another promise too. She'd solemnly sworn to actually speak to Jock Webster and ask him about Lucky and the farm, since she couldn't bring herself to visit Pig Valley on her own.

But today was the day of the hardest good-byes. This morning she, Mama and Elly had planted a rhododendron bush alongside Pa's grave. Now his favorite orange blossoms would cheer him every spring. Mama and Elly had sobbed until their eyes were puffy and red.

Not Maggie, though. It seemed as if her time of crying for Pa was over. Instead she'd gone exploring and had found another eagle feather to place in the trunk. A twin to the one that was already there.

The wind whipped suddenly at her face. She closed her eyes against it and listened. Was that Pa's laugh? His voice, floating in on the breeze? "Clean as…"

"As Lucky after his bath," she whispered. "I love you, Pa." Then she turned and called to Lucky for the very last time. "Let's go, boy."

And one last time he bounded toward her, ears flying, lips parted in that unforgettable smile. His coat was as clean as soap and water could make it (at least it had been when they'd started out from home). "Look at you," she scolded gently. She wiped a smear of dirt from the side of his nose and plucked a couple of twigs from his back. "There, that's better." She grabbed the sack that was lying at her feet and started walking toward the Pig Valley trail with Lucky trotting at her heels.

Fifteen minutes later they arrived at the farmyard. For once the pigs were actually on their feet, snouts buried in their trough, and the chickens were scrabbling over a small mound of seeds.

As if he'd been listening for their footsteps, Louie stepped out of the barn.

This was it. This was really it, thought Maggie. She felt faint, as if all the breath had been sucked from her lungs. She let the sack fall to the ground.

Chapter Twenty

For a moment no one moved. Then a shaggy shape padded out of the barn and brushed against Louie's leg. Sadie stared hard at Lucky, moved forward a few paces and sat down. Lifting her right paw, she started to wash.

Lucky nudged Maggie's leg and gazed up at her.

"Go," Maggie whispered.

As he walked toward Sadie, her paw froze in midair. Her gaze drilled into him as if she were deciding whether to flee, attack or ignore him. Finally she turned her attention back to her paw. She didn't stop washing even when Lucky sniffed at her ear.

Louie cleared his throat. "Still friends, I guess."

Maggie couldn't bring herself to speak. She gave a tiny nod.

Suddenly Lucky's tail flicked and he stared hard at the barn door. Stumbling out into the light were four tiny, fluffy kittens. Three were miniature copies of Sadie, but the fourth was a jumble of gray, white and orange.

Maggie's mouth twitched. Pa would have liked that one.

Lucky headed straight for the kittens.

Sadie streaked past him like a bolt of lightning. Back arched, fur bristling, she planted herself squarely in front of her babies. Lucky stopped dead, tucking his tail between his legs. He made a soft yelping sound.

"For Pete's sake, Sadie." Louie shook his head at her. "He ain't gonna hurt them, are you, boy?"

Lucky looked at Louie and then peered over his shoulder at Maggie. He sat down.

"See?" Louie said to Sadie. "Now be nice." Sadie's body relaxed and the ridge of fur wilted. She sat down too. A few seconds later, big-eared kitten heads poked out from either side of her body. Huge round kitten eyes peeped curiously at the world. Only one kitten moved. The spotty orange one padded forward, heading straight for Lucky.

Sadie's tail started flicking.

Lucky sat still as a fencepost.

The kitten pranced boldly up to Lucky and sniffed his paw! Slowly, carefully, Lucky bent his head and sniffed the kitten. The kitten batted his ear.

He's going to be so happy here, Maggie thought. Her eyes started to burn and she reached hastily for her sack. She untied the string, removed something from inside and marched over to Louie. She thrust the sack into his hands. "I brought Lucky's stuff," she said huskily. "The blanket he likes to sleep on, and his water pail and his ball…"

Louie gave a solemn nod.

She sucked in a breath and let it out slowly. "There's something else too." Holding out her left hand, she opened her fingers. The nugget glittered against her palm like a tiny golden sun. "I found it in the river," she said. "It's for you, to help take care of Lucky."

One side of Louie's face twisted in a frown. "D'you know how much that thing is worth?" he growled. "You keep it."

"No!" Maggie gazed pleadingly into his face. "Please, you have to take it. Pa gave me a special job to do—to take care of Lucky." Her voice trembled. "And now it's your job." She thrust her hand forward. "Here. Take it." Squinting with his good eye, Louie stared hard at her for a moment. Then he reached for the nugget and slipped it into his pocket. "I guess it'll buy a few hunks of cheese." His mouth twisted again and he gave his strange bark of a laugh.

Maggie gave a tiny smile. Louie scratched his beard. He looked over at Lucky and the kitten, then back at Maggie again. "Wait here," he said abruptly as he tramped toward the barn.

Chapter Twenty-one

Maggie walked slowly over to Lucky and knelt beside him, draping her arm around his neck. For a moment she laid her cheek against his fur, breathing in his smell for the very last time. The kitten sniffed curiously at her knee, but she ignored it. "I have to go now," she said softly. "You be a good boy and stay close to Louie. No running away." A tear slid down her cheek and plopped onto her dress.

Lucky licked her cheek. As the tears came faster and faster, he kept trying to lick them away.

Suddenly Louie was looming above her. Before she could move, he plucked the kitten from the ground and placed it gently into the box he was carrying.

A feeble mew wafted from the depths of the box.

What was he doing? Maggie swiped hastily at her eyes and stood up.

"Here." Louie thrust the box into her arms.

She almost dropped it. "What…" she cleared her throat. "What's this?" she said, gazing blindly down at the box.

The kitten mewed again, louder this time.

She blinked hard. The kitten was gazing back at her with bright blue eyes. Its mouth kept opening and closing.

Sadie's head butted hard against Maggie's shin, and she started to yowl indignantly. Then she stalked over to Louie and butted his pant leg. Back and forth, back and forth she paced, tail twitching furiously. By now Lucky had scrambled to his feet, and his nose was poking at the side of the box.

The kitten's cries grew frantic, mingling with Sadie's yowls.

"Sit," Louie ordered, pointing a finger at Lucky. Lucky sat. Louie scooped Sadie into his arms. Holding her firmly, he looked deep into her eyes. "It's okay," he said quietly. "Nothing to worry about."

Sadie gazed solemnly back at him for a moment, and then she gave a sudden wiggle. She leapt out of his arms, licked a patch of ruffled fur and padded off toward her other kittens.

Louie turned to Maggie. "She's for you."

Maggie's brain didn't seem to be working. "What?" she repeated numbly.

"To take with you."

Her mouth opened but no words came out. Take with me? To Vancouver? She stood like a statue, gaping at Louie. The kitten gave a pitiful little cry. Maggie blinked and peered into the box. "She's so tiny."

Louie snorted. "Maybe now, but she's gonna be a big one, just like her momma."

She still couldn't seem to take it in. She looked at Louie again. "But how? Why?"

"Your ma said if *he'd*," Louie jabbed a thumb at Lucky, "been a cat, your aunt would've let him come, right? Well, here's a cat."

Anger crackled through Maggie like a fast-spreading brush fire. How dare he? How dare he think that a cat, even the sweetest little orange-spotted cat, could ever take Lucky's place?

Louie was too busy lighting a cigarette to notice her scowl. He sucked in a lungful of smoke and blew it out over her head. "She'd be like a memory," he said throatily. "Of this place...of everything."

A memory? Maggie's hands clenched around the box, ready to hurl it to the ground. Or maybe she should hurl it at Louie. She didn't want a memory, she wanted Lucky. And Pa.

But she couldn't have either one of them, could she?

She peered down at Lucky, who was seated at her feet, staring intently at the box. What would he want her to do? She reached in and lifted out the kitten. Cuddling it against her chest, she tossed the box to the ground.

The kitten gave a tiny squeak, but it didn't struggle. Instead it nestled closer, rubbing its head against her neck. It was so small and as light as a dust bunny. Maggie stroked one of the orange patches and the kitten started to purr.

Louie watched them for a minute. Then he moved away, heading toward Sadie and the kittens. Slowly, carefully, Maggie knelt on the ground facing Lucky. He sniffed the kitten. His head was as big as the kitten's whole body.

She lifted his chin. "What do you think?" she whispered, staring into his eyes. "Should I take her?"

Lucky gazed back at her the way he had a million times before, eyes brimming with love.

"Should I?"

He nodded.

With a single gentle finger, Maggie stroked the silky spot on his forehead. "Thank you," she whispered. "Good-bye, Lucky." She stood up and went to get the box. She placed the kitten carefully inside it and walked over to Louie. Lucky padded behind her.

"What about Sadie?" Maggie said.

Sadie, who was lying peacefully on the ground watching her kittens, looked up at the sound of her name, but she didn't move. Not even when Lucky settled himself beside her.

"See?" Louie said. "She's fine." As they watched, one of the gray kittens clambered onto her back, perched there for an instant and tumbled off again. Sadie's eyes narrowed to slits, but she still didn't move. "She's got plenty to keep her busy. And she's got to let her go sometime. Might as well be now."

Maggie thought about that for a minute. Then she nodded. "I'm going to call her Patches."

The corner of Louie's mouth tilted up. "Good name."

She took a deep breath. "I...*we* need to get going. Mama's waiting. So I guess this is good-bye."

Louie nodded, and then he reached into the box and rubbed Patches' head. "She'll be a great mouser, you'll see. You write and tell us all about her adventures."

A picture of Louie reading her letter to Lucky and Sadie and the kittens flashed into Maggie's head. She almost smiled. "I will. Good-bye, Mr. Jenkins, and… thank you." Maggie turned and walked away without looking back.

Dianne Maycock has always wanted to write books about animals and is thrilled that her first children's book features a very special dog. Dianne currently shares her Victoria, British Columbia, home with two cats, Tiger and Ferdy, who love to steal her favorite writing chair and "read" the computer screen while she's working. *Lucky's Mountain* is based, in part, on Dianne's mother's stories of growing up in a mining town in British Columbia.